Stories to be
BOLD, BRAVE
& CONFIDENT

MOTIVATIONAL BOOK FOR BOYS AGES 6-10

★ ⋆ ★ ⋆ ★ ★ ★ ★ ★ ★ ★ ⋆ ★

BY SOPHIE POTTER

ISBN: 979-8986573755

Copyright 2022 ©

Authored by Sophie Potter

Disclaimer.

All rights reserved.

TABLE OF CONTENT

* ★ ★ ★ ★ ★ ★ ★ ★ ★ *

INTRODUCTION

Do you sometimes feel like you're living in a real-life video game? Don't worry, you're not alone. Everyone feels like that at times. Life can be active and so packed full of challenges that it's easy to make the comparison. When you're faced with a tricky obstacle in your way then in order to progress to the next level, firstly, you must learn to resolve it. This sounds easy, right? Well, sometimes it is but other times it's a bit more complicated.

We all think differently, feel differently, and act differently. There are some things we're good at, and other things that we're not so good at. There are some things we like, and other things we dislike. This is what makes each of us, us. Now, just imagine how boring the world would be if we all liked exactly the same things. There would be nothing new to discover, and no one new to meet.

Sometimes you may feel fed up because you aren't as good at certain things as your friends are. We can't be good at everything but everyone is good at something.

Being human means that we don't always get things right. We all make mistakes and sometimes the hardest part of this is admitting we were wrong. By making mistakes and moving on from them we're able to learn and grow into a brighter, happier version of ourselves.

No one is perfect but we are all unique. Being uniquely you is something to be proud of. Don't

5

let your mishaps discourage you, instead use them to learn and flourish.

In this book, you'll meet seven boys who face challenges just like you do.

Simon finds himself lost in the forest. Can he implement the new skills his grandpa taught him to find his way out?

Todd faces a tricky decision, should he compete in the tennis competition with another boy or stay loyal to his injured teammate?

Harry didn't mean to break his mom's vase. Will he take accountability for what he did and find the determination to put it right?

Dennis is baseball crazy but when his family moves house, he isn't a short walk from practice anymore. Instead, he'll have to get the bus; alone! Will he find the courage to conquer his fears?

Flynn is fed up because all his friends have found their thing, except for him. Will his curiosity and determination be strong enough to not give up his search?

Joe's new classmate doesn't like his favorite toys, so he decides he doesn't like her. After talking to his parents, can he show the respect and empathy needed to make amends with this girl and find something they both like?

Then there's Rory, when given the opportunity to cheat on his test he isn't sure what to do. Will he take the seemingly easy road to good marks or earn them through honesty and hard work?

All of these boys sometimes mess up by saying and doing the wrong things, but just like you, they all have good hearts and want to put their wrongs right. They learn new skills and life lessons along the way, and most importantly of all, they make the right decision in the end.

Life is a journey full of ups and downs. Happy moments and some sad times. New experiences and not so new. Exhilarating times and some frustrating ones. Tasty foods and some pretty gross ones. Fun with friends and disagreements. Funny conversations and spilled words. Family time and time alone. Super-fast days and relaxed slower-paced ones.

If you ever feel like you're not sure what to do, then don't forget that there's always someone to talk to, whether this is a family member or a trusted friend.

Do what you believe is right, never give up and stay strong. But most importantly of all don't be disheartened. Sometimes, in order to get to the next level, you have to take a step back and assess your mistakes. There's no hurry, you will get there in the end and when you do it'll be amazing.

SIMON TO THE RESCUE

We learn something new every day. Our minds never stop learning new information, that's pretty incredible, right?

With so much going on in our lives, sometimes it's easy to switch off and struggle to pay attention when someone tells you something.

The thing is, what this person is telling you might just be a valuable new skill that one day may just help you get out of a tricky situation.

So, the next time you have the opportunity to learn a new skill, do your best to pay attention, as you never know, it may just help you save the day.

It was a breezy but beautiful fall day and Simon was having a great time hiking through the forest with his grandpa.

After an hour of exploring the leave-trodden paths and weaving around the gnarled oak trees, grandpa instructed them to take a break.

Simon sat down on a smooth flat-faced rock and kicked his booted feet in a pile of dirt and crusted leaves.

"Here," his grandpa passed him a water bottle. "It's important to stay hydrated."

"Thanks, grandpa," Simon took it from him and took a big gulp.

"Woah, slow down else you'll get the hiccups," he chuckled.

Simon wiped his mouth onto the back of his sleeve.

Grandpa peered around him, then added. "It's also important to take note of any markers just in case you end up lost."

"A marker, what's one of those?" Simon raised an eyebrow, then he jumped to his feet.

"It's an identifiable object or landmark that can help you retrace your steps. For instance, that's a good one," grandpa pointed his hiking stick at the flat-faced rock Simon had just been sitting on.

"But that's just a rock," Simon gave him a confused look. "There are hundreds of them in this forest."

"Ah, yes but few are as flat-faced as that one is. Then there's that tree," he pointed his hiking stick at a tree with a heart and the initials B and P carved into it. "Some degenerate defaced that grand tree," he let out a sorrowful sigh, then continued. "Alas, it's a marker nonetheless."

Simon found his grandpa's words really interesting, so with curiosity, he asked him.

"Grandpa, what other tips do you have for navigating the forest?"

His grandpa immediately stopped still and cupped his ear to the sky.

"Grandpa…"

"Shush," He placed a finger to his lips.

Simon tried his best not to laugh. He didn't know what his grandpa was doing but he found it funny.

"Simon, do you hear that?"

Simon shook his head. The only thing he heard was the rustle of the leaves beneath the breeze.

"Hmm, that's because there isn't anything, well, besides this wind. But when in a survival situation I always advise you to listen. You may hear the sound of trickling water or footsteps."

"Okay grandpa," Simon smiled at him. "Can we carry on exploring now?"

"You bet we can," grandpa started to walk. "Oh! One last thing. If you ever find yourself lost then the one thing you should never do is panic. Staying calm in a crisis is the key to getting out of it."

He nodded at his grandpa, who had now started whistling an unknown tune, and waved for Simon to follow him further into the forest.

...

It was the school hiking trip to a nearby forest and Simon and his friend Duncan were very excited about it. Their teacher, Mrs. Parker gathered all of the class in a clearing in the woods and started talking to them.

"Look! Look!" Duncan whispered, as he tugged on Simon's jacket and pointed over at a tree.

Simon followed his gaze and saw a squirrel with a bushy tail scurry down the tree and dart off into the forest.

Without exchanging any words,

both boys left their group and followed the squirrel.

Eventually, they gave up trying to find it and wandered back toward their group. But after walking for a while, they still hadn't found their teacher or classmates.

"Um it is this way, isn't it?" Simon asked.

"I um, I thought it was. Oh no, we're lost," Duncan panicked.

Remembering his grandpa's advice, Simon took a deep breath, then in his calmest voice, said.

"We have to stay calm and NOT panic!"

"But what if-"

"No panicking!" Simon said assertively. "Now, let's both look for markers." He peered around him.

Duncan, who was trying his best to stay calm, rose an eyebrow at him and asked.

"Erm, Simon, what's a marker?"

"It's something easy to identify… um, like that," he pointed over at a mossy tree stump. "Have we walked past that before?"

"I don't think so," Duncan shrugged.

"Me neither, which means our group must be back this way," he pointed back the way they'd just walked from.

Both boys carried on walking through the forest. Only the further they stepped without any sign of their group; the more worried Simon became.

Duncan stopped walking and itched at his arm.

"We're lost, aren't we?" as he spoke his bottom lip quivered.

Feeling frustrated, Simon kicked his foot against the dirt and tried recalling exactly what his grandpa had told him on their last hiking trip.

"I don't understand, I did everything grandpa told me to... wait! There's one more thing. We both have to stay completely silent," Simon stayed quiet and cupped his ear so he could listen more intently.

Duncan found this very odd but he didn't dare say anything.

At first, all Simon heard were the chirps of nearby birds and the sound of his own heartbeat. He tried to block these sounds from his mind and continue to listen.

Seconds passed and so did minutes... then suddenly...

His eyes lit up in excitement when he heard something; voices.

Without saying a word, he gestured for Duncan to follow him, then he quietly walked toward the voices. Suddenly, they came to a clearing and saw their teacher and group there.

Simon and Duncan felt so relieved, as they appeared out from the trees and joined their group.

"There you are! We've all been so worried." their teacher looked at the two boys in relief.

"Sorry Mrs. Parker. We followed a squirrel but then we realized we were lost," Simon said apologetically.

"Simon helped us find our way back. He was awesome," Duncan smiled at his friend.

"Oh really. How did you do that?" the teacher asked Simon.

"I followed the survival tips my grandpa gave me. They definitely paid off in the end," he chuckled.

All of the class gathered around Simon and Duncan and asked them with excitement to explain to them what happened and how they managed to find their way back.

Simon learned a lot of important lessons that day. Firstly, he realized that straying from the group, even for a second wasn't a wise thing to do.

Secondly, he learned the importance of staying calm and showing courage in a scary situation.

And thirdly, by listening to his grandpa, even when his actions seemed funny, he'd learned some valuable new skills.

Never be afraid to show courage where needed and to put your new skills learned into practice.

So next time you have the opportunity to learn something new, take it, as you never know, one day it might just come in handy.

COLORING PAGE

(coloring with pencils is recommended)

FED UP FLYNN AND HIS UNFOUND THING

Do you have a hobby or activity that you love doing? It might be playing soccer in the park, making cardboard sculptures, or learning new tricks on your skateboard.

Maybe you don't just have one hobby you enjoy doing, instead, you might have several.

It feels awesome to have something you love doing that sparks your passion.

Sometimes people find this passion easily but other times it takes a little longer to discover it. If this is the case, then it's important to remember that your *thing* is out there somewhere but the only way of finding it is by not being afraid to try something new.

Flynn let out a loud huff and stared glumly down at his slightly nibbled piece of toast. He knew that the quicker he finished his breakfast, then the sooner dad would make him leave for school.

"Flynn, is there something wrong with your breakfast?" his dad asked him.

"I don't feel so good," he pressed his hands to his tummy. "I don't think I should go to school."

His dad gave him a questioning look, then gently asked him.

"Hmm this wouldn't have anything to do with the activity event happening today, would it?"

"No!" Flynn shook his head. "But activities
are hard and boring! Dad, please let me stay
home?"

"How can you say something is boring without
even giving it a go?" his dad tapped his hand on
Flynn's shoulder.

"All activities are boring!" he moaned out.

"That's not true. You just haven't found
the activity for you yet," he gave him an
understanding look. "Come on, you don't want to
be the last one there, do you?"

"I suppose not," Flynn grumbled.

He took a large bite out of his toast, grabbed his
backpack, then reluctantly followed his dad out
to the car.

. . .

Flynn trudged his way into the sports hall,
instantly jumping back when a girl on roller
skates zoomed past him.

"Sorry," she shouted, as she passed by.

He peered around the sports hall and then
gawped in surprise. It was jam-packed full of his
classmates partaking in different activities. He'd

never seen so many different activities happening in one place. He saw some ballerinas, tap dancers, chess players, and bean bag throwers.

Flynn had to admit that some of these activities did look exciting, so he walked over to the ping pong table where his friends Ben and Suzie were hitting the ball back and forth with their paddles.

"Please can I have a go?" he asked them.

"Sure," Suzie caught the ball in her hand, then held that and the paddle out to him.

Flynn stepped in front of the table, copied Ben's one foot to the other stance, bounced the ball on the table, and swung his paddle as hard as he could but... the ball flew off the table, across the room, and into a paddling pool of water where a group of children were floating paper boats.

Suzie went off to get the ball, then returned with wet spots on her t-shirt and a frown on her face.

"I don't think ping pongs for you," she frowned, as she took the paddle off him.

"Fine! I think it's stupid anyway," Flynn muttered under his breath.

He was still muttering to himself about how silly ping pong was as he shuffled across the room… CRASH!

He walked headfirst into his friend Chrissy, who was running around the edges of the hall.

"I'm sorry," he said to her, as he rubbed his forehead.

"That's okay," she replied, as she rubbed the side of her head. "Why aren't you doing an activity?"

"I tried ping pong but… it wasn't for me."

"Why don't you try running like me?"

Flynn liked the idea of being as fast as a superhero, so he nodded at her.

"I bet you can't catch me," she said, as she ran off.

25

Flynn hurried after her, willing for his beloved blue sneakers to carry him faster. He had almost caught up with her when suddenly he felt a niggling, gnarling, cramping pain in his side. He stopped running and pressed his hand against it.

On seeing this, Chrissy jogged over to him and asked if he was okay.

"No, there's this horrible twisting pain in my side," he groaned out.

"Oh! That sounds like a stitch. Hmm, maybe running isn't for you," she shrugged.

Flynn wasn't entirely sure what a stitch was but he decided he didn't like them, not one bit. As the pain started to subside, he mumbled goodbye to

Chrissy, then floundered over to the side of the room and leaned against the wall.

Then, suddenly, he heard music boom out, and his friend Dylan kicked out his feet, spun on the spot, then balanced himself on one hand and stuck his legs up in the air.

"What're you doing?" Flynn gave him a curious look.

"I'm breakdancing. Did you like the new move I just learned; it's called a one-hand freeze?" Dylan replied.

"It was great. Um, can you teach me how to do it?" Flynn asked him.

Dylan agreed and he showed Flynn how to balance on his hand and lift his legs.

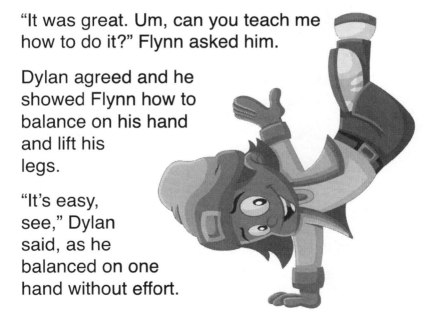

"It's easy, see," Dylan said, as he balanced on one hand without effort.

Flynn gave it a try and… trembled and quivered and then he fell in a heap on the floor.

Dylan burst out laughing, then held his hand out to help him up. Feeling embarrassed Flynn ignored Dylan's offer of help, jumped up to his feet and hurried away from him.

"See you later Flynn, I don't think breakdancing is for you," Dylan shouted after him.

All of his friends had found a hobby they loved but he didn't have anything. He didn't like ping pong, running, or breakdancing! He felt like there was nothing left for him to like.

...

When he arrived home, Flynn walked into the kitchen and let out a deflated sigh.

"Flynn, what's wrong?" his dad looked at him with concern.

"All my friends have an activity they love doing but I don't. It's not fair!" Flynn sighed.

"The only way of finding something you love is by not giving up. Do you think your friends gave up?"

"No but it's okay for them, they've all found their *thing*."

"Their *thing*?" he asked.

"Yes, everyone has a *thing* except for me."

"Flynn, the only way you're going to find your *thing*, is if you continue to try new activities."

"But I hate all of them. And I don't want to embarrass or hurt myself ever again!" Flynn exclaimed.

"Son, finding something you love isn't always easy but just think about how good you'll feel when you find it?"

"But what if I never find it?" Flynn gave him a worried glance.

"Of course, you will" he smiled encouragingly. "But only if you keep on trying and don't give up."

After that, Flynn thought a lot about his dad's words. If he didn't try to find this *thing* then he never would find it, would he? But what if he tried and tried and still didn't find it? These thoughts relentlessly swarmed around Flynn's head. He didn't have that special activity that made him happy and now he was too afraid to try and find it.

...

That weekend Flynn's friend James invited him around to play. They were having a great time watching funny animal videos when suddenly James announced that he wanted to show him something awesome. Flynn followed James outside then came to an abrupt halt. There, in the yard was a silver framed trampoline with green safety netting.

James kicked off his shoes and then climbed onto the trampoline.

"Look how high I can go?" he said, as he jumped into the air. "Come on Flynn," he waved him over.

Flynn folded his arms and shook his head. He had to admit that trampolining looked fun and he was very curious about what it would be like to go on it. But what if he jumped too high and hurt his leg? What if he fell over and James laughed at him?

He tried to put his doubts aside, and instead, remembered the encouraging things his dad had said to him. So, feeling courageous, he stood up tall, strode over to the trampoline, kicked off his blue sneakers, and then climbed onto it.

The trampoline was springy and it felt strange to step on.

"Come on Flynn, jump, it's lots of fun. Shall we do it together?"

Flynn gave a nervous nod.

"Great," James smiled. "Three. Two. One."

Flynn took a deep breath then alongside James, he jumped. The breeze ruffled his hair, and he felt weightless. He felt like he was soaring high like a bird.

This was awesome. This was incredible. This was his *thing.*

When his dad arrived to pick him up, he walked out into the yard and saw him jumping high into the air.

"Look, dad, I didn't give up and now I've found my *thing.*"

"That's great news," his dad smiled.

Please can we get a trampoline?"

"Not yet," he chuckled. "But if you like it that much then I will sign you up for trampoline lessons in town."

Flynn did one last jump, then he climbed off the trampoline, quickly put his sneakers back on, then ran over and hugged his dad.

He couldn't explain how good it felt to have found his *thing*, and he couldn't wait to start lessons and learn new moves.

He gave a fond look back at the trampoline before he left, then an even fonder look at his dad. At that moment he realized that by seeking guidance from his dad, staying curious, and not letting his doubts stop him from trying something new, he'd finally done it, he'd found his *thing*.

Life is full of new experiences and exciting opportunities. At times, these may seem scary and impossible but by taking a chance you may just open yourself up to discovering something magical.

If you ever feel nervous or worried about something, then never be afraid to ask a loved one for guidance. They might just tell you exactly what you need to hear.

COLORING PAGE

(coloring with pencils is recommended)

RORY AND THE CHEAT TEST

Do you ever wish that the answers to your big school test would magically appear in front of you? Do you want to watch cartoons instead of having to do that boring math homework?

Completing work instead of doing fun things such as drawing, playing with your friends, and riding your bike may seem unfair at times. Sometimes studying over having fun seems like the worst thing ever and you may find yourself wishing that there was a way in which you could have lots of fun but still get good grades.

If you're ever in a situation when you're not sure what to do, then just think about how good it will feel when all your hard work pays off and you get that shiny gold star on your work.

When it came to his school work then there were certain things that Rory adored. Shiny gold stars, smiley faces, a giant blue tick.

But there was one thing he wasn't so keen on… Studying! As Rory saw it, this was time that could be spent watching his favorite cartoons or riding his scooter around the park. Who wanted to spend their free time with their nose stuck in a textbook?

Rory often wished that there was a way that he could excel in his school work without having to put in any effort. If only he had a special pen that did his work for him, or an enchanted hat that when worn magicked the answers into his mind.

Then one day at school he was presented with one such opportunity. It was during a rainy break time when he was sitting at his desk doodling robots. It was as he was using a green pen to color in the robot's head, that he peered up and saw a troublesome boy named Danny peering at something on the teacher's desk.

Rory continued drawing, then he heard the croak of a voice. He looked up to see Danny peering over him.

"Look what Miss Clearwater left on her desk," Danny gave a quick flash of his ink-scribbled hand. "Seems that I have the answers to tomorrow's big test. Come find me if you want them."

Rory chewed on the side of his lip in thought. Tomorrow's big test was all about pond life. Rory didn't care much for learning about frogs and water plants, not when he could be having fun instead. He looked over at Danny, who was now jotting the answers from hand to page.

Then suddenly a girl with pigtails skipped over to Danny and exchanged a purple lollipop for a scrap of paper.

Rory stared down at his drawing and sighed. He didn't want to cheat but he didn't want to fail either.

He peered over at Danny who was now sharpening his pencil over the trashcan. As he watched him a boy in a stripy red top walked over to him and placed a candy bar in his hand in exchange for a piece of paper.

Rory doubly sighed. It seemed that everyone had the answers to the test apart from him. At this rate, he'd be the only one to have a sad face on his work instead of a smiley one. With this in mind, he gripped his green pen tightly in his hand, scraped back his chair, then marched over to Danny and asked him.

"Please can I have the answers?"

"Sure," Danny waved a piece of paper in front of him. "They're all yours. But… you have to give me something first."

Rory stared down at his hand, pondered on this, and then held the green pen out to him. Danny snatched it off him and placed the scrunched-up piece of paper there instead.

"It's a pleasure doing business with you. Come and thank me when you get a gold star."

Rory nodded, then walked back over to his desk. He stuffed the answers into his pencil case and then stared down at his robot doodle which was now three-thirds green.

Break time ended and class continued. As Miss Clearwater talked to the class all Rory could think about was that bit of scrunched-up paper in his pencil case. The thought of it being there caused his tummy to swish and gurgle.

…

When Rory arrived home, having the answers for the big test played on his mind. He thought about them while tidying away his toys, while eating his dinner, and while helping his dad do the dishes. Then his dad said to him.

"Rory, finish your homework then you can go and watch cartoons."

He gulped back. He was going to tell him that he didn't have any homework but however hard he tried the lie refused to come out.

"Is something wrong?" he gave him a quizzing look.

"I-I have the answers to the test tomorrow," he spluttered out. "I traded my green pen for them but I don't know what to do. I don't want to cheat but I don't want to fail either."

His dad led him over to the kitchen table, sat down next to him, and calmly said.

"Tell me, do you think it's right to cheat?"

Rory shook his head.

"But I don't want to be the only one to get a sad face on my work."

40

"Son, if you just look at the answers without putting any of the hard work in and by being dishonest, then do you think you deserve the reward?"

Rory shook his head again.

"No, dad. I haven't looked at the answers yet; honest. I don't know what to do."

"Only you can decide that," he patted his arm. "I just hope that you make the right decision."

His dad left the room, leaving Rory to stare at his pencil case in thought. In the end, he opened it, pulled out the piece of paper with the answers on it, marched over to the trashcan, and threw it inside.

He didn't want to do well through cheating. He wanted to do well because he deserved to. So, Rory took out his school books and started revising for his test. When he'd finished his head was filled with all the information he needed and he felt pleased with himself for putting in all this hard work.

His dad walked into the room while he was packing away his books.

"I'm proud of you Rory, it's not always easy to make the right choice."

"It's the only way I'm going to earn a gold star," he smiled. "Besides, turns out pond life isn't actually that boring. Did you know that frogs have four life cycle changes?"

"No, I didn't know that," his dad grinned.

Feeling positive about all of the hard work he'd put in; Rory went and watched some cartons before bedtime.

...

The next day at school when the test was about to start, he noticed Danny look over at him and give him a thumbs up. Rory ignored him and clutched his pen in his hand. He was determined to keep focused and do his best on the test.

Miss Clearwater asked the first question: "Name three different types of plants commonly found in a pond?"

Numerous groans sounded out throughout the room, and Rory turned to see Danny looking confused. Rory smiled to himself, he knew the answer to this question, so he quickly wrote down waterlilies, water lettuce, and the cardinal flower.

The questions continued and Rory found that thanks to all his hard work he knew all of the answers. Afterward, the teacher set them some work to do while she marked the tests.

Before she handed the results back to them, she had an announcement: "Children, some of you

43

may have found those questions were different than expected. I left a set of false answers on my desk to see if any of you would be tempted to use them." She stopped in front of Danny's desk and placed down his test full of red crosses and a sad face drawn on it. "Cheating is never the answer. Good grades should be earned through hard work."

When she stopped at Rory's desk he was shaking with nerves. Then she smiled and passed him back his test paper, there, on it was a shiny gold star, a smiley face, and a giant blue tick.

Rory felt so pleased with himself but then he remembered what he did, and the guilt niggled away at him. Taking a deep breath, he said.

"Miss, I did take the answers but I didn't look at them. Instead, I spent hours studying. I'm sorry for even thinking about cheating, I know that was wrong."

The teacher gave a serious look at first but then her mouth turned into a warm smile.

"Rory, it's tempting to take the easy route sometimes. The important thing is that you chose the right decision in the end, not only that but you were also honest with me about what you did and that wasn't an easy thing for you to do. So, you deserve that high mark, well done."

She peered around the class.

"As for the rest of you, those of you that decided to cheat can join me at break time for an extra study lesson."

Groans and moans ensued but not from Rory. He was still smiling as he proudly looked down at his result.

That break time he walked past Danny and the other cheaters who were remaining there for their punishment. The girl with the pigtails grumbled at Danny to give her back her purple lollipop and the boy in the stripy red top groaned that he wanted back his candy bar.

Rory went outside and took out his robot drawing which was still partly colored in green. He took out a yellow pen and colored the rest in with that. Then he sat back and admired both his artwork, and his hard-earned shiny gold star, smiley face, and giant blue tick.

Sometimes in life, we face many scary challenges. Taking the easy route and being dishonest may seem tempting but if you follow your heart, put in the hard work, and do what you believe is right then it's sure to work out just fine in the end.

COLORING PAGE

(coloring with pencils is recommended)

47

JOE'S DILEMMA

If you were to write a list of all of your favorite things, what would be on it?

Perhaps you like watermelon-flavored sweets, the color emerald green, digging a hole at the beach, watching cartoons, going down the waterslide, visiting the park, and eating ice cream?

49

If you don't like these things then don't worry. Every single person is unique, and they all have their own favorites list.

If someone doesn't like the same things you do or share the same views on something as you, then this is okay. We all think differently and like different things.

Stay true to what you like and who you are, and remember to always be kind to your classmates, even if they have different likes to you. This means no pulling weird faces if they eat something you find gross or teasing them for liking a song you think is silly.

Your friends liking what they like makes them, THEM. Being you and liking what you like makes you, YOU.

It was Joe's first day of school and he was very excited about it. He'd spent ages that morning choosing which of his favorite collectible figures he should take in to show his class. He eventually settled on the falcon in a gold-buttoned jacket, and a bear wearing a feathered hat which he carefully placed in each pocket of his shorts.

In class, during their free time, Joe spotted a girl called Mia sitting alone and coloring in an outline of a dinosaur. With a smile on his face, he sat down next to her, then took his figures out of his pockets and proudly placed them on the table.

"This one's called Bruno, it's really rare," he moved the falcon figure. "And this one's called Sid. It's not as rare but I still like him," he made the bear do a little dance.

"That's nice," Mia said, without looking up from her coloring.

"Yeah, these toys are really cool. You can play with them if you want?" he held both of the mini figures out to her in his open palm.

"No thanks," she said, as she continued coloring in her picture. "I don't like them that much. I prefer coloring."

"You DON'T like THEM?!" Joe stared at her in shock. "B-but EVERYONE likes them. They're the coolest toy EVER!"

"Not me," she shook her head.

"B-but they're too awesome not to like."

"I still don't like them," she shrugged.

"How can you NOT like them?" he gawped at her.

"Not sure, I just think they're kind of dumb," she gave him an apologetic look and then carried on coloring.

Joe felt the rage whirl through his body, so he stuffed his figures back in each pocket, scraped back his chair, and clambered to his feet.

"I think you're the dumb one," he yelled.

"I, um, I just like what I like," she said in a timid voice.

"But everyone else likes them, so you must be silly and really weird!" Joe huffed at her, then he stormed off across the classroom.

By the time his parents picked him up from school he felt even angrier than before. He didn't understand why Mia didn't like something so cool and popular. He concluded she wasn't a nice person and he never wanted to see her ever again!

He got into the back of the car with a sour face and folded arms.

"Joe, what's wrong? Didn't you have a good day?" His mom peered around her seat and looked at him with concern.

"NO!" He shook his head. "I had a terrible day! There's a girl in my class called Mia and I hate her!"

"Joe, hate isn't a very nice word to use about someone," his mom gave him a quizzing look. "What did Mia do to upset you so much?"

"She doesn't like my figures and refused to play with them. She said they're dumb. Well, I say she's dumb! I hate her and I'm not talking to her ever again," he huffed out.

"Oh!" his mom exclaimed. "That seems a little unfair. You and I don't always like the same things but we still get on, don't we?"

Joe thought about this, then grumbled.

"I suppose. But you don't hate my figures, do you?"

"No, I don't hate them but I do think I'm a little too old to love them either," she chuckled. "I'd much prefer to spend my free time gardening but you don't like doing that, do you? You say it's boring."

"But it is boring. But my figures are cool… everyone my age likes them; except for *her*!"

"Well, I don't dislike you just because you think gardening is boring," mom said.

"Your mom's right. I don't like those romantic movies she enjoys watching but this doesn't mean I don't like her," his dad chuckled from the driver's seat. "And unlike you, I can't stand tomato sauce but this doesn't mean I dislike you, does it?"

"I suppose not," Joe stuck out his bottom lip. "But I think my figures are cool."

"Joe, we can still like different things and have different views on something and still get along. It's our differences that make us unique," Dad said.

The more he thought about his mom and dad's words, the more he realized that Mia not liking his figures didn't matter. He suddenly felt a swirling feeling in his tummy on knowing that he'd been mean to her, and he longed to put things right.

The next day during free time in class, Joe saw Mia deep in concentration as she colored in the outline of a rocket. So, keeping his figures safely in his pockets, he walked over to her and sat down next to her.

"I like rockets," he peered down at the picture she was coloring.

"Yes, me too," she looked up and smiled at him, then she continued with her coloring.

"I'm sorry for calling you silly and weird. It's okay that you don't like my figures. It's okay to like different things," he said.

"Okay. Um, thanks," She peered up at him with a nervous smile. "Do you want to color with me?" she held a red crayon out to him.

"Sure. I like coloring too," he grinned as he took the crayon off her.

"Good. You can color in the top of the rocket," she pointed down at the picture.

Joe and Mia had lots of fun coloring together. They were both very proud of their finished picture and the teacher complimented it and let them both pick a sticker from the sticker sheet. When Mia picked a sticker that Joe didn't like, he didn't say anything mean about it, instead, he just smiled at her.

When Joe's parents picked him up from school, he proudly showed them the orange star sticker he'd stuck on his sweater. Even better than receiving the sticker was that despite their differences, he was now friends with Mia.

In fact, he was looking forward to returning to school tomorrow so he could play with her again.

We all think differently, feel differently, and act differently. This means that your favorite color might not be the same as your classmates', and your all-time favorite food might be different from theirs too.

It's important to always respect and show empathy toward others, even if their likes and opinions aren't the same as yours.

Always remember, it's your differences that make you, YOU.

And there's only one YOU in the entire world.

COLORING PAGE

(coloring with pencils is recommended)

DENNIS AND THE DAUNTING JOURNEY

We all have things we enjoy that we feel comfortable doing. These might be family days out, playing soccer in the park, or riding around the neighborhood on your scooter.

Being able to do the things we like feels great. But sometimes we have to do things that make us feel nervous and afraid to be able to get to the fun things.

Perhaps you don't like traveling in the car? Maybe there's a scary dog you have to pass by to get to the playground? Or you might have a very talkative neighbor that likes to chatter with you for ages whenever they see you.

Sometimes in life, we have to take ourselves out of our comfort zone and do things we don't really enjoy doing.

If you don't show courage and do the things you feel nervous about doing, then you'll never get to experience the fun stuff.

Dennis leaned on his baseball bat and stared glumly at the "sold" sign in front of him. Suddenly, a gust of wind blew his baseball cap off his head and whirled it through the air. He gasped in shock and tried clawing at the air to get it back.

His dad swooped over, caught the cap in his grip, then placed it down on Dennis's head.

"Come on son, we better get going," his dad placed his arm around Dennis's shoulders and then led him across the front yard.

When Dennis reached the car, he took one look back at his former home before he let out a solemn sigh, then stepped into the back of the vehicle.

To Dennis, this wasn't just a house. It was the place of birthdays past, from a magnificent magician to a vivid green dinosaur cake.

It was the place of first words and enchanting stories.

It was the place where bat swings were perfected and his passion for baseball grew.

Dennis slumped down in his seat and stared glumly out of the window as they drove away from the home he adored. The worst part about the move was that his new neighborhood wasn't a short walk away from where his baseball team practiced anymore. Instead, it was a whole bus journey away.

For Dennis, the thought of having to get on a bus all alone terrified him. What if he lost his ticket? What if the bus was really busy and he had to sit next to a stranger? What if he got off on the wrong stop?

The more Dennis thought about this the more he reached the same conclusion… the only way to avoid the dreaded bus journey was if he left the baseball team forever!

…

Dennis looked around his new room, then gathered up his lucky baseball, his team cap, his baseball shirt, glove, and his bat, and he placed them all in a cardboard box. He carried the box into the kitchen as his mom was cooking dinner, and he left it down onto the table.

"Dennis, why is this here?" his mom peered down into the box, then gave him a confused look.

"I don't need it anymore. I'm leaving the team," he declared with a sigh.

"You're leaving the team? But Dennis, you love being a part of that team," she looked at him with concern.

"Yeah, I do. But I don't live near it anymore and I don't want to get the bus all alone. I might get lost or have to sit by a stranger," he groaned.

His mom took his lucky ball out of the box and held it out in front of her.

"I remember when you caught this ball and won your team the match. You were so excited and, on the walk home you told me one day you were going to become a professional baseball player."

His mom passed him the ball, then said. "Sweetie, do you really want to give that up?"

"No," he took the ball off her and examined the slight scratches and scuffs on it that told of games past. "B-but now we live miles away from practice."

His mom gave this some thought, then suddenly the corner of her lips curled into a gentle smile.

"How about this weekend we go on a practice journey together? That way you will know where to buy a ticket, what to say, and which stop to get off at."

"Yes. Okay," Dennis gave a slight nod.

As he placed the ball down into his box of baseball items, he knew in his heart that he truly didn't want to give up the hobby he loved the most. He still wasn't sure if he'd ever be brave enough to get the bus alone but he decided that a practice run with his mom was at least worth a try.

...

The following Saturday, as promised, his mom came with him to the bus station. It was very noisy here and there were so many different buses with various numbers on them. Dennis instantly found himself feeling overwhelmed but his mom took his hand and led him over to a ticket machine.

"You want to get a return ticket for the number 10 bus to Queens Village. You can choose this option here," she pressed her finger by the screen.

With his mom's guidance, Dennis managed to select his ticket destination, then he slotted in the coins, and collected his ticket.

"Great," his mom smiled at him. "Now we need to find the spot where our bus is leaving from. Any ideas?"

Dennis peered around him, then pointed when he saw a sign with the numbers 8-10 on it and a big blue arrow beneath it.

"This way," he started walking in the direction of the arrow. "There's number 10," he rushed over to the designated seating area and planted himself down on one of the plastic chairs.

"Great work, Dennis," his mom said, as she sat down next to him.

When the number 10 bus pulled into the station, he joined the queue, then he stepped up to the bus driver. With his ticket clutched tightly in his hand, he looked back at his mom who gave him a reassuring nod. Then he took a step forward, smiled at the bus driver, then handed him his ticket.

"Thank you," the driver smiled. Then he checked the ticket and handed it back to him. "Here you go, young man."

"Thank you," Dennis replied, as he took his ticket off him, then hurried over to a free seat.

His mom showed her ticket to the driver, then she came over and joined Dennis.

"You're doing really well," she patted his arm.

As the bus started on its route Dennis stared out of the window and tried to concentrate. Each of the stops seemed to blur into one and before he realized what was happening, his mom was giving him a gentle nudge on the arm.

"Dennis, look," she pointed over to the screen close to the driver, where the words *Next Stop: Queens Village* were shown in red.

Dennis gulped back, gripped onto the side of his seat, and waited anxiously for the bus to stop.

Then he quickly got up, hurried toward the door, and then stepped off the bus.

"See," his mom said, as she walked up to him. "You can do it. Now, how about we go and get a milkshake before we get the bus back?"

"Yes please," Dennis replied.

That journey had seemed easy but then his mom had been with him. Everything seemed less scary when he wasn't alone. The thought of doing that journey by himself made his tummy gurgle and his throat turn dry. He couldn't even enjoy his chocolate milkshake properly because he was so nervous about doing the bus trip alone.

...

The big day arrived and Dennis's mom gave a kiss on the cheek and told him to remember each step he needed to do. As both of his parents waved him off, he waved back at them, readjusted his cap, then gently swung his baseball bat alongside him as he walked toward the bus station.

Doubts still niggled away at his mind and he kept on wondering if he should just turn around and go home. He tried not to think about his worries and instead he concentrated on what steps he needed to take.

He went up to the ticket machine, chose his destination, slotted in the coins, waited for his ticket, then walked over to the number 10 waiting area. As he sat there, he held firmly onto his ticket and stared down at his bat.

When the bus arrived, he nervously joined the queue. By the time he reached the front, he was so anxious his legs were shaking like jello. Taking a deep breath, Dennis smiled at the driver and passed him his ticket. The driver checked it, then waved him onward.

Dennis slowly walked along the bus aisle and desperately tried to scope out a good seat to sit at. That's when he spotted Jake, the captain of his baseball team, he was sitting near the front by himself and he had his baseball bat gripped in between his knees. He'd always admired Jake but he didn't know him all that well.

Feeling brave, he took a deep breath then walked over to Jake and sat down next to him.

"Hi Jake, so you get this bus to practice too?" Dennis asked him.

"Oh, hi Dennis. Yeah, I do," he smiled at him. "I've not seen you on it before."

"No, I've just moved house so this is my new route," he gave a nervous smile back.

"Oh! Cool," he replied.

Both boys soon started talking to each other and the time seemed to zoom by. Soon their stop came into view and both boys hopped off the bus and went to practice.

From that day onward, Dennis wasn't afraid of getting the bus alone anymore. Instead, he looked forward to sitting next to his friend Jake and talking to him on the journey.

Although change can seem scary at times, Dennis was glad that he hadn't let his worries overcome him and cause him to give up baseball. Now, thanks to his courage, he was not only still part of his baseball team but he'd also made a great new friend in Jake.

In life we face many different challenges, some of these may seem exciting and some may seem frightening.

Sometimes it may seem easier to give up doing something you love over being taken out of your comfort zone but in the end, all this will do is make you miserable.

Giving up on something you enjoy doing because you're nervous and apprehensive will just make you feel sad and regretful in the long run.

But by being brave and making yourself do that scary thing, not only will you feel super pleased with yourself but it may also lead to unexpected positives.

COLORING PAGE

(coloring with pencils is recommended)

SMASH, CRASH AND HARRY

Do you ever get Mad? I mean really, really, want to scream at the top of your lungs and stamp your feet mad?

We all feel like this sometimes, and in our temper, we may end up saying something bad to someone we care about or end up breaking something we didn't mean to.

Admitting you were in the wrong can be hard at times but it's also the right thing to do. Taking accountability for what you did, then having the determination to never give up until you've fixed your mistake will show your family and friends just how much you care.

Harry peered under his bed, emptied his toybox, and looked in his wardrobe… but no matter how hard he searched he couldn't find his favorite toy truck anywhere!

He thudded downstairs and ran along the hallway.

"Mom, I can't find my toy truck," he groaned. "You know, the white one with the bright green wheels. Can you come to help me look for it?"

"Harry, I'm cooking at the moment. I'm sure it'll show up." His mom said as she peered around the kitchen doorframe with a wooden spoon in hand.

Harry searched beneath the couch cushions and looked behind the goldfish bowl but he still couldn't find it. Feeling more and more frustrated he puffed out his cheeks, flailed out his limbs, and yelled.

"Mom, help me look for it. I want it now!" He stomped his feet in frustration, then continued to poke around the room… SMASH!!!

Harry gulped back in guilt as he stared down at his mom's beloved mustard-colored porcelain vase, three jagged pieces from its top left-hand corner now broken off next to it on the floor.

On hearing the commotion his mom rushed out of the kitchen, stopping abruptly as she looked from Harry to the broken vase.

"W-what happened?" her eyes began to tear up.

"N-nothing, I-I, I didn't mean it."

Without saying a word his mom disappeared into the kitchen, then reappeared soon after with a dustpan and brush. She shooed Harry away from the broken pieces and crouched on her hands and knees to sweep them up.

When Harry's dad saw what was going on, he took the dustpan and brush off mom, and gently told her that he'd sort this out. She walked off with glazed-over eyes and a sad composure.

"Harry, did you break this?" Dad looked directly at him.

"I-I don't know."

"This is mom's favorite vase that Aunt Isabelle gifted her before she moved away. She put it out ready for her birthday tomorrow, as Aunt Isabelle always sends her flowers to go in it. Now she won't be able to use it."

Harry folded his arms and stuck out his bottom lip. He felt terrible for breaking the vase and for upsetting his mom the day before her birthday but he didn't think there was anything he could do to fix it; the vase was broken.

Feeling overwhelmed with guilt he ran past dad and went down to the bottom of the garden. He kicked the ground in his frustration then slumped down onto the grass. That's when he saw it hidden behind the flower bed; his white truck with the bright green wheels.

He was turning the toy truck over in his hands when his grandpa shuffled over to him.

"Hi Harry, why the glum face?"

Harry blew air up at his forehead, then turned the toy truck over in his hand.

"I was searching for my toy truck and I accidentally broke mom's special vase. Now she'll be sad on her birthday."

"Now, now," grandpa gave a shake of his head. "It's not so bad, we all make mistakes, hey, even I've made a fair few in my time."

"Really?" Harry looked up at him in surprise.

"Oh, yes. In my old wisdom, I've learned that the important thing is to take responsibility for your mistakes and to do your best to fix them."

Harry gave this some thought, then replied.

"But the vase can't be fixed. It's too damaged."

"Are you sure about that?" he gave him a questioning look. "In my experience, I've learned that there's usually a way. In this case, I'd say it's effort and glue."

Harry contemplated on this. He really wanted to make amends for his actions but it seemed so hard to do.

"B-but it's her birthday tomorrow. There's not enough time."

"Pfft! Time," grandpa chuckled. "Trust me, Harry, there's always time if you choose to make some."

Harry gave this some thought, then he nodded at grandpa in agreement. He knew he could either sit out here and feel sorry about how he'd disappointed his parents, or he could do his best to fix his mistake.

After that, the two of them shut themselves away in the garage, and complete with the dustpan and brush containing the broken vase pieces, and some glue, Harry did his best to make amends for his mistake and fix his mom's favorite vase.

Harry found that holding the pieces in place while grandpa glued them caused his hand to ache, and he had an itch on the tip of his nose that he couldn't scratch.

"There, all done," grandpa moved his hand away from the vase.

Harry let go of it but before he could let out a cheer in success, the broken pieces fell off the vase and tumbled onto the table.

"I can't do it. It's impossible!" Harry huffed out as he leaped to his feet.

"Nonsense!" his grandpa replied. "We just need my special glue, that's all. Wait here."

Grandpa shuffled out of the garage and reappeared a few minutes later waving a small tube about. He sat down and started reading the glue instructions.

"That will never work. It's useless," Harry sighed.

"Alas, I'm afraid nothing easy is ever worth doing. If you choose to just give up… then so be it," he placed the glue down on the table, then headed toward the door.

Harry thought about how sad his mom looked, and then he thought about how upset she'd be tomorrow on her birthday when Aunt Isabelle's flowers arrived but she didn't have her special vase to put them in.

"Grandpa, wait!" Harry announced. "Let's do this."

Grandpa smiled to himself as he walked back over to the table. It took Harry and grandpa lots of time, patience, and three snack stops but finally, they managed to glue all the pieces back together.

Now, as Harry held onto the top side of the vase, he found himself too afraid to let go of it in case it fell apart again.

"Harry, you can't hold it forever. You've got to let go."

"B-but what if the pieces fall off?" he gave a concerned look.

"Then we'll just glue them back on," grandpa shrugged. "Come on Harry, you have to take a risk."

Harry knew his grandpa was right. So, he held his breath as he slowly inched his hand away from the glued-on vase pieces. He stared at the vase with wide eyes and a sweaty palm.

The pieces didn't fall off. They'd successfully fixed the vase.

"Thanks grandpa, it looks as good as new," Harry said excitedly.

"See, I told you we could do it. My special glue never lets me down," his grandpa grinned.

Harry smiled proudly at his grandpa. Fixing the vase had taken a lot of time, patience, and determination but seeing the finished result sure felt good.

...

The next morning Harry woke up extra early and rushed downstairs to wish his mom a happy birthday. She thanked him but he noticed the sad look in her eyes as she opened a box containing the beautiful bouquet from Aunt Isabelle.

As his dad walked into the room with a huge Happy Birthday balloon, Harry said.

"Mom, I'm sorry I got mad about finding my toy truck and for accidentally breaking your vase."

He passed his mom a carefully wrapped-up present and watched as she peeled back the paper and, on seeing the fixed vase, her sadness transformed into a wide smile.

"You did this, for me?" she looked at the vase in surprise.

"Yep. Grandpa helped me with the gluing but I worked out where all of the pieces went and held them in place," Harry gave a gleeful nod. "It was my mistake, and I wanted to put things right."

His mom burst into tears but this time they were happy ones.

"This is the best birthday present I could have wished for. Thank you, Harry," she hugged him.

Then his dad ruffled his hair and gave him a high-five. Fixing his mistake has been hard work and time-consuming but seeing how pleased it made his parents meant that it was well worth it.

Harry smiled as he watched mom arrange the flowers in the vase and then display them in the living room window. Now, everyone that passed by outside could see the colorful flowers in the as-good-as-new vase.

Everyone makes mistakes sometimes, and that's okay. By making these mistakes we can learn from them and grow as a person. The important thing is that we take account of our actions, however hard this might be, and that we do our best to put things right.

COLORING PAGE

(coloring with pencils is recommended)

83

TODD AND THE TRICKY CHOICE

Decisions, decisions. Life is full of them...

Some are easy to make while others are on the trickier side.

When faced with a hard-to-make decision you might find yourself struggling to decide what to do.

85

If this is the case, then don't worry, you aren't alone. Asking a family member or a friend for advice can be really helpful.

If you're still not sure then it's always a good idea to think about how your decision will affect other people, and how you would feel if you were them.

Whatever decision you make, it's important to think about the feelings of any others involved and to do what you feel is right.

For Todd, nothing in life was more enjoyable than having maple syrup pancakes for breakfast, browsing through his coin collection, family board game nights…

And most importantly of all, playing tennis with his best friend Lee.

When it came to tennis, Todd and Lee made the perfect duo. They were so good that they'd made it to the finals of the local contest.

Todd was sure that with his powerful right swing and Lee's quick serves they were sure to win. In fact, Todd was so certain of this that he'd even cleared space on his desk for the trophy.

In preparation for the big match, their coach made them practice extra hard. They both found all of these extra sessions exhausting and sweaty but they didn't grumble about it at all, as they both really wanted to win.

During their final practice session, Todd swung his racket at the ball and hurled it toward his coach, who was on the other side of the court. His coach darted to reach it, then hit it back over the net. Lee leaped forward and stretched out his arm…

"Ow! Ow! Ow!" Lee knelt on the court and clutched his arm to his chest.

Both Todd and their coach rushed over to him and asked him what was wrong.

"It's my wrist, it really hurts," Lee whimpered.

The coach led Lee off to see the physio. When he returned, he told Todd that Lee had sprained his wrist and would be out of action for at least a couple of weeks.

"B-but the competition is two days away," Todd said in a panicked voice.

"Sorry Todd but Lee needs to give his wrist time to heal properly before he plays again," the coach said.

"So that's it. All our hard work was for nothing," Todd sighed.

"Not necessary. You could compete in the finals with Jack instead."

Todd peered over at a nearby court where Jack was effortlessly hitting the ball. Jack was a talented player and if they teamed up in the final, they had a good chance of winning.

"But what about Lee?" Todd asked his coach.

"I'm sure Lee will understand," he patted his shoulder. "It seems a shame you have to miss out on the final when you've put all that hard work in."

Todd felt very confused. A part of him really wanted to be rewarded for all of his hard work and to compete in the finals but the other part of him didn't feel right competing without Lee.

He told his coach he'd think about it and let him know in the morning.

When Todd arrived home, he felt more conflicted about this than before. He wandered into the kitchen, sunk onto a chair, and sucked on his bottom lip. He was so lost in thought he didn't notice his older brother Steve come into the room.

"Todd, what's wrong?" he asked him.

"It's Lee, he's sprained his wrist and can't play the finals. Coach wants me to team up with Jack instead but I got this far with Lee, and I don't want him to feel like I've abandoned him. I don't know what to do," Todd said sadly.

"Hmm that sounds like a hard choice," Steve grabbed an apple out of the fruit bowl, threw it in the air then caught it in one hand. "Sounds to me like you should follow your heart and do what you believe is right."

"But I don't know what I should do," Todd said.

Steve took a big bite out of the apple, chewed on it, then continued.

"If you compete in the match and you win with Jack, how would you feel about it?"

Todd gave this question some serious thought.

"Um, I think I'd feel bad about it. I don't want to win with Jack, I want to win with Lee."

"It looks like you've reached your answer," Steve grinned at him, then took another bite out of the apple as he left the room.

The next morning Todd told his coach that he didn't want to compete in the competition without Lee. Although Todd felt sad about not competing, he knew in his heart that sticking by Lee was the right thing to do.

...

Todd excitedly hurried onto the court with his racket. Today was the day that Lee was returning to practice. He rushed over to his friend and welcomed him back but he couldn't help but notice how nervous Lee looked.

Then, when Todd hit the ball his way, he immediately hopped to the side to avoid it.

Todd just thought Lee was a little rusty and needed some more practice. But as the training session continued so did Lee's strange behavior. He ducked out of the way of the ball, tangled his racket in the net, and refused to serve.

As the practice session came to an end, Todd walked over to his friend and looked at him with concern.

"Lee, what's wrong? Why aren't you playing like you usually do?" Todd asked him.

"I don't want to injure myself again," Lee anxiously scratched his arm. "I, um, I don't think I want to play tennis anymore."

"But you love tennis. You can't give it up because of one setback," he stared at him in confusion.

"It's no good. I'm afraid of the ball now. Maybe you should team up with Jack instead?" he sighed.

Todd shook his head. He didn't want to team up with Jack, he wanted to stay loyal to Lee. They made a great team and he didn't want to lose him.

"Leave it to me. I'll help you get your confidence back," Todd reassured him.

"You will?" Lee arched his brow.

"Yep, I sure will," he told him.

After that, Todd did his best to help Lee regain his confidence. They threw the ball at each other, chased each other around the net, and practiced swinging their rackets mid-air. Then, gradually over time, Lee found that he wasn't afraid of hurting himself anymore and because of all of his practicing his serves became stronger than ever.

Their coach entered them into a local competition and thanks to all of their hard work, teamwork, and practice they won.

As Todd let out a whoop of delight, he realized that this win meant far more to him than any of his previous ones. He looked over at Lee's grinning face and knew that winning through loyalty to a friend was so much better than winning for the sake of winning.

If like Todd, you're ever faced with a difficult decision and you're not sure what you should do then it's best not to dwell on it in silence.

Discussing how you feel with a loved one is a great way to find clarity.

The right decision isn't always the easiest one to make…

But if you do what you believe is right then you'll know in your heart that you made the correct choice.

COLORING PAGE

(coloring with pencils is recommended)

IMPRINT

The author is represented by Silviyas Books LTD

Publishing imprint Silvis Books

Contact: info@silvisbooks.com

Publication Year: 2022

ISBN: 979-8986573755

Cover illustration: Christina Michalos

Interior images from www.depositphotos.com

Responsible for printing: Amazon Kindle Direct Publishing

Made in the USA
Monee, IL
13 November 2022

17695483R00055